The Story of AND

The Little Word That Changed the World

Sandy Eisenberg Sasso

Illustrated by Joani Keller Rothenberg

With a song by Carrie Newcomer

flyaway books

There once was a girl who loved to count.
She counted the cracks in the sidewalk,
the clouds in the sky, and the stars at night.
Most of all, she loved to count
the word *and* in every story she read.

"What a waste of time," said her neighbor.

"Be serious," said her principal.

"Stop dillydallying," said her parents.

She couldn't convince anyone that counting *and* wasn't silly, until the day she started reading an old story — and everyone listened.

Down a dusty road, a circle rolled along,
feeling all alone with all its edges gone.
Then Circle bumped into a single line.
Could this somehow be a secret sign?
But Line thought Circle was a wreck.
"You don't even have a neck!"

But over the hill came the small word AND,
so simple and sure, saying, "Yes, we can!"

She joined their hands. "Together you'll bloom into a glowing red balloon.

"When you gather more than three, what a party it will be!"

Triangle sat alone on the ground,
making all her very angled sounds.
A rectangle scooched up with a grumbling noise.
"You're a silly almost-trapezoid!"
She was hurt by what he said,
and she scratched her pointy head.

But over the hill came the small word AND,
so simple and sure, saying, "Yes, we can!"

She joined their hands.
"There is no flaw.
Together, you can be a seesaw.

One side goes up, and one goes down.

And many seesaws make a playground!"

Once there was a solitary square,
thumping along as quickly as he dared.
Triangle slid up, all full of pride,
saying, "Hey, you have a useless side!"
Square was stung by what she said,
and he almost turned and fled.

But over the hill came the small word AND,
so simple and sure, saying, "Yes, we can!"

She joined their hands. "Have no doubt.
The two of you can build a house.
And then many houses could
together be a neighborhood!"

Line went marching down the street,
so very proper and so very neat.
When he saw Oval in a flower bed,
he laughed and said,
"You're such an egghead!"
Oval acted mad, mad, mad,
but inside she was simply sad.

Then over the hill came the small word AND,
so simple and sure, saying, "Yes, we can!"

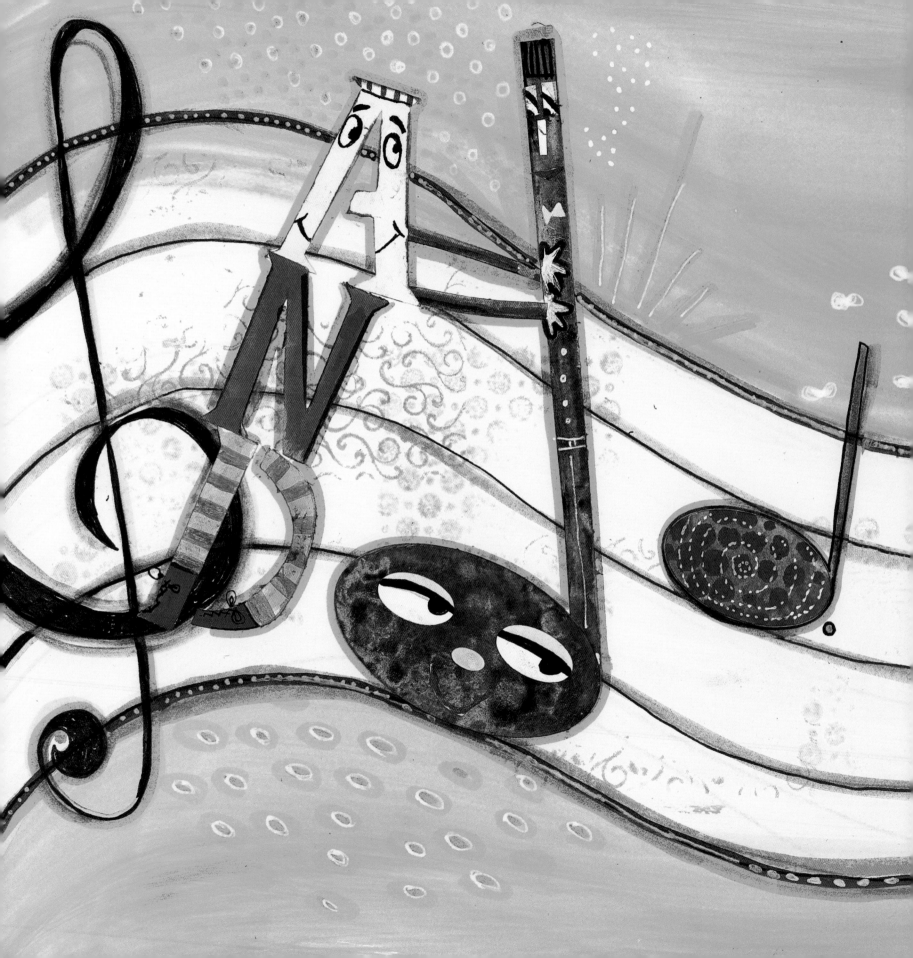

Octagon sat upon a mat
and tipped his little eight-sided hat.
A cylinder rolled up to one side.
"You couldn't rock and roll if you tried!"
Octagon really got upset.
Those words made him start to fret.

But over the hill came the small word AND,
so simple and sure, saying, "Yes, we can!"

She joined their hands. "You are able!
The two of you can be a table.
And when people gather round,
a new community is found!"

To create a world without a missing piece,
all the different shapes make us complete.
I am I, and you are you.
This is really nothing new.
But remember, it's a fact:
We are stronger back to back to back.

When we meet someone different from us
and we are tempted to make a fuss,
look for our friend the small word AND,
so simple and sure, saying, "Yes, we can!"

She joins our hands and shows us how to trust.

Then you and I can become us.

What wonders there can be

when you and I are we ... family!

To download an original song by singer/songwriter Carrie Newcomer, visit www.flyawaybooks.com/resources.

For Dennis AND Debbie AND Brad AND Ari AND Levi AND David
AND Darwin AND Naomi AND Raven—who have changed my world
—S. E. S.

For Jeff AND Leela AND Ben Tamir AND Maya AND Tal
—J. K. R.

Text © 2019 Sandy Eisenberg Sasso
Illustrations © 2019 Joani Keller Rothenberg

First edition
Published by Flyaway Books
Louisville, Kentucky

19 20 21 22 23 24 25 26 27 28—10 9 8 7 6 5 4 3 2 1

Book design by Alexandra Segal and Allison Taylor
Text set in Trade Gothic LT Std

Library of Congress Cataloging-in-Publication Data
Names: Sasso, Sandy Eisenberg, author. | Rothenberg, Joani Keller, 1964- illustrator. | Newcomer, Carrie, songwriter.
Title: The story of and : the little word that changed the world / written by Sandy Eisenberg Sasso ; illustrated by Joani Keller Rothenberg ; with a song by Carrie Newcomer.
Description: First edition. | Louisville, Kentucky : Flyaway Books, [2019] | Summary: A young girl who enjoys counting the word "and" in each story she reads relates a tale of shapes that are contentious until "and" brings them together.
Identifiers: LCCN 2018036656 (print) | LCCN 2018042009 (ebook) | ISBN 9781611649154 (ebook) | ISBN 9781947888050 (hbk.)
Subjects: | CYAC: And (The English word)--Fiction. | Shape--Fiction. | Cooperativeness--Fiction.
Classification: LCC PZ7.S24914 (ebook) | LCC PZ7.S24914 Sto 2019 (print) | DDC [E]--dc23
LC record available at https://lccn.loc.gov/2018036656

PRINTED IN CHINA

Most Flyaway Books are available at special quantity discounts when purchased in bulk by corporations, organizations, and special-interest groups. For more information, please e-mail SpecialSales@flyawaybooks.com.